Enid Blyton

A FARAWAY TREE
ADVENTURE

The Land of
ENCHANTMENTS

For Sophia and Cece
A. P.

HODDER CHILDREN'S BOOKS
Text first published in Great Britain as chapters 16-19 of *The Folk of the Faraway Tree* in 1946
First published as *A Faraway Tree Adventure: The Land of Enchantments* in 2017
by Egmont UK Limited
This edition published in 2021 by Hodder & Stoughton Limited

3 5 7 9 10 8 6 4 2

A CIP catalogue record for this book is available from the British Library.

ISBN 978 1 444 95992 5

Printed and bound in China

The paper and board used in this book are made from wood from responsible sources.

Hodder Children's Books
An imprint of
Hachette Children's Group
Part of Hodder & Stoughton
Carmelite House
50 Victoria Embankment
London EC4Y 0DZ

An Hachette UK Company
www.hachette.co.uk
www.hachettechildrens.co.uk

Enid Blyton

A FARAWAY TREE
ADVENTURE

The Land of
ENCHANTMENTS

HODDER

The World of the FARAWAY TREE

MOON-FACE lives at the very top. In his house is the start of the **SLIPPERY-SLIP**, a huge slide that curves all the way down inside the trunk of the tree.

SILKY lives below Moon-Face. She is the prettiest little fairy you ever did see.

SAUCEPAN MAN is a funny old thing. His saucepans make lots of noise when they jangle together, so he can't hear very well

CHAPTER ONE
The Land of Secrets

Connie could not forget the exciting Faraway Tree, and the different lands that came at the top. She asked the others about all the different lands they had been to, and **begged and begged them** to take her to the next one.

'We'll see what Moon-Face says,' said Joe at last. 'We don't go to every land, Connie. You wouldn't like to go to **the Land of Whizz-About**, for instance, would you? Moon-Face once went there, and he said he couldn't bear it – everything went at such a pace, and he was out of breath the whole time.'

'Well, I think **it sounds rather exciting**,' said Connie, who was intensely curious about everything to do with the different lands. 'Oh, Joe, let's find out what land is there next. I really must go.'

'All right,' said Joe. 'We'll ask Mother if we can have a day out tomorrow, and **we'll go up the tree** if you like. But mind – if there is a horrid land, we're not going. We've had too many narrow escapes now, to risk getting caught somewhere nasty.'

Mother said they could go up the tree the next day. 'I'll give you sandwiches, if you like, and you can **have lunch in the wood** or up the tree, whichever you like,' she told them.

'**Oh, up the tree!**' cried Connie. So, when the next day came, she wore old clothes without even being told! She was learning to be sensible at last.

They set off soon after breakfast. They hadn't let Silky or Moon-Face know they were coming, but they felt sure they would be in the tree.

Up they climbed. The Angry Pixie was sitting at his window, which was wide open. He waved to them, and Connie was glad to see he had no ink or water to throw at her.

'**Going up to the Land of Secrets?**' he shouted to them.

'Oh – is the Land of Secrets there?' cried Joe. 'It sounds exciting. What's it like?'

'**Oh – just secrets!**' said the Angry Pixie. 'You can usually find out anything you badly want to know.'

'I'd like to know some secrets too,' said Connie.

'**What secrets do you want to know?**'
asked Joe.

'Oh – I'd like to know how much money
the **old man who lives next door** to us at
home has got,' said Connie. 'And I'd like to
know what Mrs Toms at home has done to
make people not speak to her – and . . .'

'**What an awful girl you are!**' said Beth. 'Those are other people's secrets, not yours. Fancy wanting to find out other people's secrets!'

'Yes, it's not nice of you, Connie,' said Frannie. 'Joe, don't let Connie go into the Land of Secrets if that's the kind of thing she wants to find out. **She's gone all curious and prying again, like she used to be.**'

Connie was angry. **She went red and glared** at the others. 'Well, don't you want to know secrets too?' she said. 'You said you did!'

'Yes, but not other people's,' said Joe at once. 'I'd like to know **where to find the very first violets for instance**, so that I could surprise Mother on her birthday with a great big bunch. They are her favourite flowers.'

'And I'd like to know the **secret of curly hair**, so that I could use it on all my dolls,' said Beth.

'And I'd like to know the secret of **growing lettuces with big hearts**,' said Frannie. 'Mine never grow nice ones.'

'What silly secrets!' said Connie.

They **climbed up to Silky's house**, but the door was shut. They went up to Moon-Face's, but his door was shut too. The Old Saucepan Man was not about and neither was Watzisname. Nobody seemed to be about at all.

'We might as well go up into the Land of Secrets, and find the others, and **have our picnic with them**,' said Frannie.

They all went up the topmost branch, and up the yellow ladder through the hole in the cloud, and then into the Land of Secrets.

It was a **curious land, quiet, perfectly still**, and a sort of twilight hung over it. There was no sun to be seen at all.

'It feels secret and solemn!' said Joe, with a little shiver. 'I'm not sure if I like it.'

'**Come on!**' **said Beth**. 'Let's go and find
the others and see how we get to know secrets.'

They came to a hill, with several coloured
doors in it, set with sparkling stones that
glittered in the curious twilight.

'They must be the doors of caves,' said Joe.

'Look! – there are names on the doors.'

The children read them. They were peculiar names. '**Witch Know-a-Lot**.' 'The Enchanter Wise-Man.' 'Dame Tell-You-All.' 'Mrs Hidden.' '**The Wizard Tall-Hat**.'

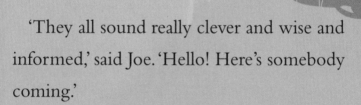

'They all sound really clever and wise and informed,' said Joe. 'Hello! Here's somebody coming.'

A tall fairy was coming along, carrying a pair of wings. She stopped and spoke to the children.

'Do you know where Dame Tell-You-All lives, please? I want to know how to fasten on these wings and fly with them.'

'**She lives in that cave,**' said Beth,
pointing to where a door had 'Dame Tell-You-
All' painted on it in big letters.

'Thank you,' said the fairy, and rapped sharply on the door. It opened and she went inside. It shut. In about half a minute it opened again, and out came the fairy, this time with the wings on her back. She rose into the air and flew off, waving to the children.

'The Dame's really clever!' she cried. 'I can fly now. Look!'

'This is an exciting place,' said Beth. 'Goodness, the things we could learn! **I wish I had a pair of wings**. I've a good mind to go and ask Dame Tell-You-All how to get some, and then how to fly with them.'

'**Look!**' said Joe, suddenly. There was Saucepan Man, his pans clashing as usual.

'Saucepan, WHERE ARE SILKY AND MOON-FACE?' said Joe.

'Don't know,' said Saucepan, 'and **don't shout at me** like that. I haven't seen Silky or Moon-Face today.'

'Let's have our picnic here, and then go and see if **Silky and Moon-Face have come home**,' said Joe. 'Somehow I don't think we'll go about finding out secrets. This land is a bit too mysterious for me!'

But Connie made up her mind she would find a few secrets! She would **have a bit of fun** on her own.

They all sat down on a flowery bank. It was still twilight, which seemed very odd, as Joe's watch said the time was half past twelve in the middle of the day. As they ate, they watched the different visitors coming and going to the cave on the hillside.

The children talked to everyone who passed. It was peculiar, the different secrets that people wanted to know. One grumpy-looking pixie wanted to know **the secret of laughter**.

'I've never laughed in my life,' he told Joe. 'And I'd like to. But nothing ever seems funny to me. Perhaps the Enchanter Wise-Man can tell me. **He's very, very clever.**'

The Enchanter plainly knew the secret of laughter because, when the grumpy-looking pixie came out of the cave he was smiling. **He roared with laughter** as he passed the picnicking party.

'Such a joke!' he said to them. '**Such a joke!**'

'What was the secret?' asked Connie.

'Ah, that's nothing to do with you!' said the pixie. '**That's my secret, not yours!**'

A very grand fairy came flying down to the hillside. She looked rich and powerful and very beautiful. Connie wondered what secret she had come to find out. **It must be a very grand secret indeed**. The fairy did not tell the children what she wanted to know. She smiled at them and went to knock on Mrs Hidden's door.

CHAPTER TWO
Connie Gets into Trouble

Connie slipped away unseen. She was
longing to know what secret the
beautiful fairy wanted to find out. It
must be a very powerful secret.
If only she could hear it!
Perhaps if she listened outside Mrs
Hidden's door, she might catch a few words.
She went off very quietly, and
climbed a little way up the hillside

to where she had noticed Mrs Hidden's door.

There it was – a pale green one, striped with red lines and a curious pattern. It was open!

Connie crept up to it. She could hear voices inside.

She stood in the doorway and **peeped inside**. There was a winding passage leading into the hill from the doorway. She crept down it. She turned a corner and found herself looking into a very curious room. It was small, and yet it looked very, very big because when Connie looked at the corners they faded away and weren't there.

It gave her an uncomfortable feeling, **as if she was in a dream**.

Connie heard the secret that the beautiful fairy wanted to know, and she heard Mrs Hidden give her the answer. Connie shivered with delight. It was a very wonderful and powerful secret.

Connie meant to use it herself! She began to creep out of the cave.

But her foot caught against a loose stone in the passage and it made a noise. At once Mrs Hidden called out in a sharp voice: '**Who's there?** Who's prying and peeping? Who's listening? **I'll put a spell on you**, I will! If you have heard any secrets, you will not be able to speak again!'

26

Connie fled, afraid of having a spell put on her. **She came rushing down the hillside**, very frightened. The others heard her and frowned.

'**Connie!** Surely you haven't been after secrets when we said you were not to try and find out anything?' began Joe.

Connie opened her mouth to answer – but not a word came out! **Not a single word!**

'**She can't speak**,' said Watzisname. 'She's been listening at doors and hearing things not meant for her ears. I guess old Mrs Hidden has put a spell on her. Serve her right.'

Connie opened her mouth and tried to speak again, **pointing back to the cave** she had come from. Saucepan got up in a hurry.

'I can see what she means to say,' he said to the others. '**She's been caught prying and peeping**, and she's afraid Mrs Hidden will come after her. She probably will as soon as she has finished with that beautiful fairy who went into her cave. **We'd better go**. Mrs Hidden is not a nice person to deal with when she is angry.'

They all ran to the hole, and got down it as quickly as possible

'Hey – **do you think Silky and Moon-Face are still up there** in the Land of Secrets?' asked Beth.

But they weren't, because as they came down the branch to Moon-Face's house, they heard voices, and saw Silky and Moon-Face undoing shopping parcels.

Silky looked at Connie in sympathy.

'Poor Connie! Whatever can we do about it? We'll have to wait till the Land of Enchantments comes, and then go up and find someone who can take the spell away. **I don't know how to make you better**.'

'Never mind, Connie,' said Beth, seeing that Connie looked really upset. 'As soon as the Land of Enchantments comes, we'll take you there and **have you put right!**'

CHAPTER THREE
Three Important Rules

Mother was **surprised and very concerned**, to find that Connie couldn't speak.

'We'd better take her to the doctor,' she said.

'Oh no, Mother, that's no use,' said Joe. 'It's a spell that Mrs Hidden put on Connie for hearing something she shouldn't have listened to. Only another spell can put her right.'

'When the Land of Enchantments comes we will take Connie there, and see if we can find someone who will give her her voice back again,' said Beth.

'She'll have to be patient till then,' said Frannie.

Three days went by, and **no news came from the tree folk**. Then old Mrs Saucepan arrived, with a basket full of lovely new-made cakes for them.

'The **Land of Enchantments** will be at the top of the tree tomorrow,' Mrs Saucepan said.

Everyone sat up. '**What, so soon?**' said Joe. 'That's a bit of luck for Connie.'

'It is,' said old Mrs Saucepan. 'Still, there are plenty of lands where she might get her voice put right. You'll have to be a bit careful in the Land of Enchantments, though. **It's so easy to get enchanted there**, without knowing it.'

'**Whatever do you mean?**' said Mother, in alarm. 'I don't think I want the children to go there, if there is any danger.'

'I'll send Saucepan with them,' said the old lady. '**I'll give him a powerful spell**, which will get anyone out of an enchantment if they get into it by mistake. You needn't worry.'

'Oh, that's all right then,' said Joe. '**I didn't want to get enchanted**, and have to stay up there for the rest of my life!'

'You must remember one or two things,' said Mrs Saucepan. 'Don't step into a ring drawn on the ground in chalk. Don't stroke any black cats with green eyes. **And don't be rude to anyone at all**.'

'We'll remember,' said Joe. 'Thank you very
much. Cheer up, Connie – you'll soon get
your voice back!'

The next day it was raining, and Mother
didn't want the children to go up the Tree.
But **Connie's eyes filled with tears**, and
Mother saw how badly she wanted to go.

'Well, put on your raincoats,' she said, 'and take umbrellas. Then you'll be all right. It may not be raining in the Land of Enchantments. And do remember what Mrs Saucepan said, Joe, and be very careful.'

'We'll be careful,' said Joe, putting on his old raincoat. 'No treading in chalk rings – no stroking of black cats with green eyes – and no rudeness from anyone!'

Saucepan and Silky were at Moon-Face's house waiting for the children to come.

'Is the **Land of Enchantments** up there?' said Joe, nodding his head towards the top of the tree.

'It must be,' said Silky. '**I've met two witches and two enchanters** coming down the tree today. They don't live here, so they must have come down from the Land of Enchantments.'

Joe turned to Saucepan. '**Did your mother give you a powerful spell** to take with you, Saucepan, in case we get caught in an enchantment?'

'**Uh-oh!**' groaned Saucepan, beginning to look all round him in a hurry. '**Where did I put it?** Silky, have you seen it? What did I do with it?'

'**You really are a silly, Saucepan,**' said Silky, looking everywhere. 'You know it's a spell that can move about. It's no use putting it down for a minute, because it will only move off somewhere.'

The spell was found at last. It was a **funny round red spell**, with little things that stuck out all round it rather like spiders' legs. It could move about with these, and had walked off Moon-Face's shelf, and settled itself down at the edge of the slippery-slip.

'**Look at that!**' said Saucepan, snatching it up quickly. 'Another inch and it would have been down the slippery-slip and gone for ever. Where shall I put it for safety?'

'In a kettle and put the lid on,' said Joe. So **into a kettle went the spell**, and the lid was put on as tightly as could be.

'It's safe now,' said Saucepan. 'Come on, up we go, and be careful, everyone!'

CHAPTER FOUR
In Search of a Spell

They all left their umbrellas and raincoats behind, and went up into the Land of Enchantments. It wasn't a twilight land like the Land of Secrets; it was a land of strange colours and lights and shadows. **Everything shone and shimmered and moved**. Nothing stayed the same for more than a moment. It was beautiful and strange.

There were curious little shops everywhere where **witches, enchanters and goblins** cried their wares. There was a shining palace that

looked as if it was made of glass, and towered up into the sky. **The Enchanter Mighty-One** lived there. He was head of the whole land.

There were magic cloaks for sale, that could make anyone invisible at once. How Joe longed to buy one! There were silver wands full of magic. There were enchantments for everything!

'**Spell to turn your enemy into a spider,**' cried a goblin. 'Spell to enchant a bird to your hand! Spell to understand the whispering of the trees!'

'Oh, **look at all those fairies** dancing in a ring and singing as they dance!' said Beth, turning her head as she saw a party of bright-winged fairies dancing in a ring together.

She went over to watch them, and they smiled at her and held out their hands. '**Come and dance too, little girl!**' they cried.

Beth didn't see that they were **all dancing inside a ring** drawn on the ground in white chalk! In no time she was in the ring too, linking hands with the fairies and dancing round and round!

The others watched, smiling. Then Joe gave a cry of horror, and pointed to the ground.

'**Beth's gone into a ring!** Beth, come out, quick!'

45

Beth looked alarmed. She dropped the hands of the fairies, and came to the edge of the ring.

But oh dear, **poor Beth couldn't jump over it!** She was a prisoner in the magic ring.

'Saucepan, get out the spell at once, the one your mother gave you!' cried Joe. **'Quick, quick!** Before anything happens to Beth. She may be getting enchanted.'

Saucepan took the lid off the kettle where he had put the spell. He put in his hand and groped around. **He groped and he groped**, a worried look coming on his face.

'Saucepan, be quick!' said Joe.

'The spell has gone!' said Saucepan miserably. 'Look in the kettle, Joe – the spell isn't there. I can't get Beth out of the magic ring!'

Everyone stared at Saucepan in horror.

'Saucepan! **The spell can't be gone!** Why, you put the lid on as tightly as can be,' said Silky. '**Let me look!**'

Everyone looked, but it was quite plain to see that the kettle was empty. **There was no spell there**.

'Well, maybe you didn't put it into that kettle, **but into another one**,' said Joe. 'You've got so many hanging round you. Look in another kettle, Saucepan.'

So Saucepan looked into every one of his kettles, **big and small**, and even into his saucepans too – but that spell was not to be found.

'We're in real danger in this strange land, **without a spell to protect us**,' said Silky. 'But we can't run off home because we mustn't leave Beth in a magic ring, and we have to try and get Connie put right. Oh dear!'

'**We'll have to find someone** who will get Beth out of the ring,' said Joe anxiously. 'Let's go round the Land of Enchantments and see if anyone will help us.'

So they started off, leaving poor **Beth looking sadly** after them. But the fairies took her hands and made her dance once again.

The children came to a small shop where a **goblin with green ears and eyes** sat at the back. In front of him were piled boxes and bottles of all sorts, some with such strange spells in them that they shimmered as if they were alive.

'**Could you help us?**' said Joe, politely.
'Our sister has got into a magic ring **by mistake**, and we want to get her out.'

The goblin grinned. '**Oh, no**, I'm not helping you to get her out!' he said. 'Magic rings are one of our little traps to keep people here.'

'**You're a very nasty person then**,' said Moon-Face, who was upset because he was very fond of Beth.

The goblin **glared at him** and moved his big green ears backwards and forwards like a dog.

'**How dare you call me names?**' he said. 'I'll turn you into a voice that can do nothing but call rude names, if you're not careful.'

'**Indeed you won't**,' said Moon-Face, getting angry. 'What, a silly little goblin like you daring to put a spell on me, Moon-Face! You think too much of yourself, little green goblin. **Go and bury yourself in the garden!**'

'Moon-Face!' said Frannie, suddenly. '**Don't be rude**. Remember what Mrs Saucepan said.'

But it was too late. Moon-Face had been rude and **now he was in the goblin's power**. When the little green goblin beckoned to him, poor Moon-Face found that his legs took him to the goblin, no matter how he tried not to go.

'You will work for me now, Moon-Face!' said the goblin. **'Now, just sort out those boxes** into their right sizes for me. And remember, no more rudeness.'

Frannie burst into tears. She couldn't bear to see Moon-Face having to work for the nasty little goblin. 'Oh, Saucepan, **why did you lose that spell?**' she wailed. 'Why did you?'

'Here's a powerful-looking enchanter,' said Joe, as a tall man in a great flowing cloak swept by.

'**Maybe he could help us**.'

He stopped the enchanter and spoke to him. **A black cat** came out from the tall man's shimmering cloak, and strolled over to Silky, blinking its green eyes at her.

'**Can you help us, please?**' asked Joe, politely. 'Some of our friends are in difficulties here.'

He was just going on to explain, when he suddenly stopped and ran at Silky who was **stroking the black cat** and saying sweet things to it! She was very fond of cats, and stroked every one she saw. **But she mustn't** – she mustn't do that in the Land of Enchantments!

It was too late. She had done it. Now she had to follow the enchanter, who smiled at them. '**A nice little fairy!**' he said to them. 'I shall like having her around with the black cat. She will be company for him. She can take care of him.'

To the great dismay of the others, the enchanter swept off, taking poor Silky, his cloak flowing out, covering her and the cat.

'**Oh, now Silky's gone!**' sobbed Frannie. 'First it was Beth, then Moon-Face, and now Silky. Whatever are we going to do?'

CHAPTER FIVE
Lost and Found

'**Look!**' said Saucepan, suddenly, and he
pointed to a little shop nearby. On it was
painted a sentence in yellow paint:

'**COME HERE TO GET THINGS YOU HAVE
LOST!**'

They went over to it, Frannie still wiping her
eyes. The shop was kept by the same beautiful
fairy who had flown to Mrs Hidden's cave, and
whose secret Connie had overheard!
Connie was afraid of going to her, but

Saucepan pulled her over to the shop.

The beautiful fairy knew Saucepan, and was delighted to see him. When he told her about Connie, she looked grave. '**Yes, I know all about it**,' she said. 'It was my secret she heard, and a very wonderful secret it was. Has she written it down to tell any of you?'

Connie shook her head. She took out her little notebook and wrote in it. She tore out the page and gave it to the fairy.

'I am very sorry for what I did,' the fairy read. '**Please forgive me**. I haven't told the secret, and I never will. If you will give me back my lost voice, I promise never to peep and pry again, or to try and overhear things not meant for me.'

'**I will forgive you**,' said the fairy, gravely. 'But, Connie, if you ever tell the secret, I am afraid your voice will be lost again and will never come back. Look! I will give it back to you now – but remember to be careful in future.'

She handed Connie a little bottle of blue and yellow liquid, and a small red glass. 'Drink what is in the bottle,' she said. '**Your voice is there**. It's a good thing I didn't sell it to anyone.'

Connie poured out the curious liquid and drank it. **It tasted bitter**, and she pulled a face.

'Oh, how horrid!' she cried, and then clapped her hands in delight. '**I can speak!** My voice is back! Oh, I can talk!'

'**It's a pity!**' said Saucepan. 'I like you better when you don't talk. Still, I needn't listen.'

Connie was so excited at having her voice back again that she talked and talked without stopping. **The others were very silent.** Both Joe and Saucepan were worried, and Frannie was still crying.

'Be quiet, Connie!' said Joe at last. 'Saucepan, **WHAT SHALL WE DO?**'

'Go back and **ask my mother for another spell**,' said Saucepan. 'That's the best thing I can think of.'

So they all went back to the hole in the cloud. But they couldn't get down it because there were so many people coming up!

'**The Land of Enchantments must be moving** away again soon,' said Saucepan, in dismay. '**Look!** Everyone is hurrying back to it, with their toadstools and things!'

'**We can't risk going down** to your mother then,' said Joe, more worried than ever. 'If the land moves on it will take Moon-Face, Beth and Silky with it, and **we shall never see them again**.'

They sat down at the edge of the hole, and looked worried and upset. **Whatever were they going to do?**

Then Frannie gave such a loud cry that everyone jumped. 'What's that? **What's that sticking out of the spout of that kettle, Saucepan?** Something red, waving about – look!'

Everyone looked – and Saucepan gave a shout. '**It's the spell!** It must have crawled up the spout, and that's why we didn't see it when we looked in the kettle! It couldn't get out because the spout is too small. Those are its leg-things waving about, trying to get out of the spout!'

'Quick! Get it out, Saucepan,' said Joe.

'**Bad spell, naughty spell**,' said Saucepan severely, and poked his finger into the spout, pushing the spell right back. **It fell with a little thud** into the inside of the kettle. At once, Saucepan took off the lid, put in his hand and grabbed the spell. He jumped to his feet.

'**Come on!** Maybe we've just got time to rescue the others, Beth first!'

They rushed to the magic ring, and
Saucepan stepped into it with the spell
held firmly in his hand. At once the chalk ring
faded away, the fairies ran off and **Beth was
free**. How she hugged Saucepan!

'No time to waste, **no time to waste**,' said
Saucepan, and ran off to find Silky. He saw
the enchanter in his floating cloak, talking to a
witch, and rushed up to him.

'**Silky, Silky, where are you?** I've a spell
to set you free!' cried Saucepan.

The enchanter looked down and saw the
wriggling red spell in Saucepan's hand.
He shook out his cloak and Silky appeared.
Saucepan took her by the hand.

'Come on! You're free. You don't need to
follow him any more. He's afraid of this spell.'

The enchanter certainly was. **He ran off
with his black cat without a word**.

'Now for Moon-Face,' said Saucepan. 'Gosh, **can I hear the humming noise** that means this land will soon be on the move?'

He could, and so could the others. With beating hearts, they **rushed to the green goblin's shop**. There was no time to waste. Saucepan threw the red spell at the goblin, and it went down the back of his neck.

'You're free, Moon-Face. **Come quickly!**' cried Saucepan. '**The land is on the move!**'

Moon-Face rushed after the others, leaving the goblin to try and **grab the wriggling spell**. Everyone rushed to the hole that led down through the cloud. The land was shaking a little already, as if it was just going to move.

Beth and Frannie were pushed down quickly.
Then Silky and Connie followed, **almost
falling down in their hurry**. Then came
Moon-Face and Joe, and last of all Saucepan,
who nearly got stuck in the hole with his
saucepans and kettles. He got free and fell
down with a bump.

'**The land's just off!**' he cried, as a
creaking sound came down the ladder. 'We
only just escaped this time! Gosh, look how
I've dented my kettles!'